LAMBTON COUNTY LIBRARY

C3

2 0210 00384812 5

D0922873

JUL 0 9	DATE DUE	

WITHDRAWN

j 398.2 HEL c.3
Helmer, Marilyn
Three barnyard tales

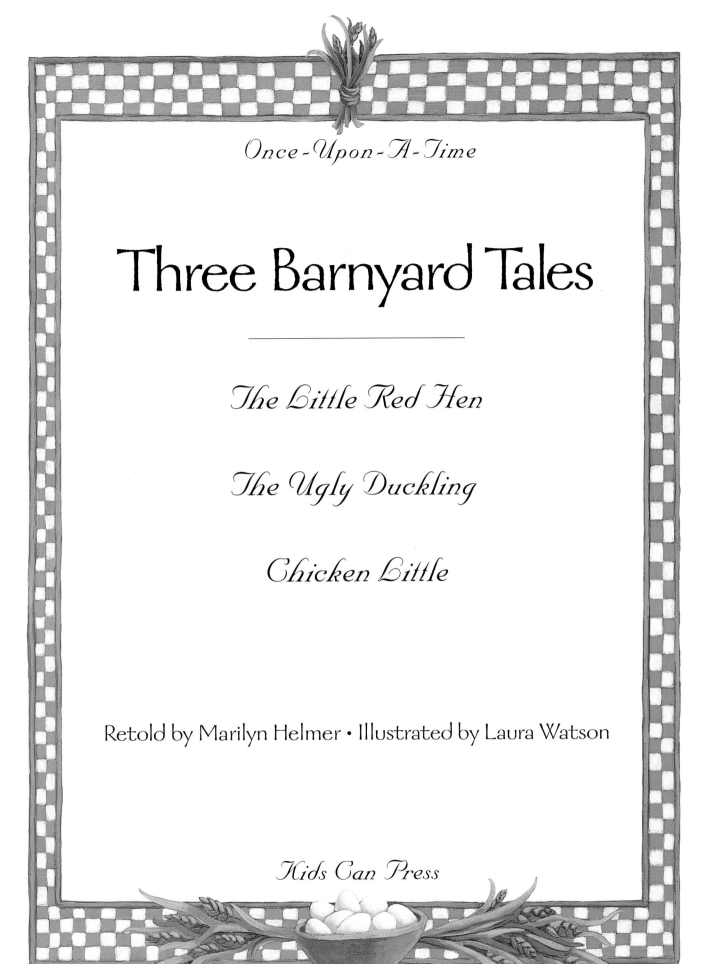

Once-Upon-A-Time

Three Barnyard Tales

The Little Red Hen

The Ugly Duckling

Chicken Little

Retold by Marilyn Helmer • Illustrated by Laura Watson

Kids Can Press

LAMBTON COUNTY LIBRARY, WYOMING, ONTARIO

To my childhood friend, Brenda Fisher Lewington — there's laughter in heaven. — M. H.

For Doris Amy Wilkinson, with love. — L. W.

Text © 2002 Marilyn Helmer
Illustrations © 2002 Laura Watson

All rights reserved. No part of this publication may be reproduced, stored in a retrieval system or transmitted, in any form or by any means, without the prior written permission of Kids Can Press Ltd. or, in case of photocopying or other reprographic copying, a license from CANCOPY (Canadian Copyright Licensing Agency), 1 Yonge Street, Suite 1900, Toronto, ON, M5E 1E5.

Kids Can Press acknowledges the financial support of the Ontario Arts Council, the Canada Council for the Arts and the Government of Canada, through the BPIDP, for our publishing activity.

Published in Canada by
Kids Can Press Ltd.
29 Birch Avenue
Toronto, ON M4V 1E2

Published in the U.S. by
Kids Can Press Ltd.
2250 Military Road
Tonawanda, NY 14150

www.kidscanpress.com

The artwork in this book was rendered in acrylic.
The text is set in Berkeley.

Series editor: Debbie Rogosin
Editor: David MacDonald
Designer: Marie Bartholomew
Printed in Hong Kong by Wing King Tong Company Limited

This book is smyth sewn casebound.

CM 02 0 9 8 7 6 5 4 3 2 1
C.3

National Library of Canada Cataloguing in Publication Data

Helmer, Marilyn
    Three barnyard tales

(Once-upon-a-time)
Contents: The little red hen — The ugly duckling — Chicken Little.
ISBN 1-55074-796-7

1. Fairy tales. I. Watson, Laura, 1968-   . II. Title. III. Series: Helmer, Marilyn. Once-upon-a-time.

PS8565.E4594T454 2002   j398.2   C2001-930665-2
PZ8.H3696Th 2002

Kids Can Press is a Nelvana company

Contents

The Little Red Hen

One fine fall day, the little Red Hen was scratching about in the barnyard. To her delight, she found some grains of wheat.

"What luck!" said the little Red Hen. "If I plant these grains, they'll grow into wheat. Then I can grind the wheat into flour and bake a delicious loaf of bread."

On the same farm lived a Cat, a Duck and a Pig. They spent their days doing as little as possible. The Cat napped for hours in any sunny spot she could find. The Duck paddled lazily around the pond and the Pig lay in his sty, wallowing in the mud.

The little Red Hen showed them what she had found. "If we plant these grains, they'll grow into wheat. Then we can grind the wheat into flour and bake a delicious loaf of bread," she said. "Who will help me plant them?"

"Not I," meowed the Cat, with a great big yawn.

"Nor I," quacked the Duck, swimming quickly away.

"Nor I," grunted the Pig, peeking out of his mud puddle.

"Then I'll do it myself," said the little Red Hen. She planted the grains in a sunny spot next to the barnyard fence.

Soon fall turned to winter and snow covered the ground. Beneath the earth, the grains of wheat lay safe and dry.

Months passed and the weather grew warmer, melting away the snow. Every day the little Red Hen checked the spot where she had planted the grains.

One bright spring morning, the little Red Hen noticed tender green shoots poking through the earth. From then on, she watered and weeded the wheat every day until it was ripe and ready to be harvested.

"Who will help me cut the wheat?" asked the little Red Hen.
"Not I," meowed the Cat, cleaning her whiskers.

"Nor I," quacked the Duck, as she dove deep into the pond.

"Nor I," grunted the Pig, snuffling in his trough.

"Then I'll do it myself," said the little Red Hen. She cut the wheat and gathered it up. Now it was time to separate the grain from the stems.

"Who will help me thresh the wheat?" asked the little Red Hen.

"Not I," meowed the Cat, curling up in the sun.

"Nor I," quacked the Duck, as she ruffled her feathers.

"Nor I," grunted the Pig, rooting about in the muck.

"Then I'll do it myself," said the little Red Hen. She beat the wheat with a stick. Once all the grain was off the stems, she put it in a sack. Now it was ready to take to the mill to be ground into flour.

"Who will help me carry this heavy sack?" asked the little Red Hen.

"Not I," meowed the Cat, with a flick of her tail.

"Nor I," quacked the Duck, flapping her wings.

"Nor I," grunted the Pig, rolling onto his back.

"Then I'll do it myself," said the little Red Hen. She carried the heavy sack to the mill. When the miller had ground the grain into flour, the little Red Hen carried the sack home again.

Back at the barnyard, the little Red Hen mixed the flour with sugar and eggs and shortening and yeast. She put the dough into a pan and placed it in the oven. Soon, a most delicious smell wafted across the barnyard. First the Cat caught a whiff of it. Then the Duck noticed it, too. The Pig raised his head, sniffed the air and smacked his lips. When the bread was done, the little Red Hen opened the oven and pulled out the big crusty loaf.

"Now," said the little Red Hen. "Who will help me eat the bread?"

"I will!" meowed the Cat. Quick as a flash, she leapt to her feet and dashed toward the little Red Hen.

"I will!" quacked the Duck. She hopped out of the water and waddled right behind the Cat.

"Me too!" grunted the Pig. He scrambled from his puddle, splashing mud in all directions, and hurried after the Duck.

"Not a chance!" said the little Red Hen. "I planted the grains all by myself. I cut and threshed the wheat all by myself. I carried the heavy sack to the mill and back all by myself. I baked the flour into bread ALL BY MYSELF! And that is how I'm going to eat it!"

With that, the little Red Hen ate the delicious crusty loaf right to the very last crumb — all by herself.

The Ugly Duckling

Once long ago, in a barnyard by an old farmhouse, a mother duck sat patiently on her nest, waiting for her eggs to hatch. Six of the eggs were alike, but the seventh was larger and heavier than the rest.

The mother duck had been sitting for such a long time that she began to wonder if the eggs would ever hatch. Finally she stood up to stretch. As she did, she heard a cracking sound. One after another, the eggs began to break open. One, two, three, four, five, six downy yellow ducklings popped out. The seventh egg was slower to hatch. When it did, out stumbled a large gray chick with straggly feathers.

"Goodness me!" exclaimed the mother duck. "That one doesn't look like a duckling at all. I wonder if someone put a turkey egg in my nest."

The next morning she led the ducklings to the river. "Everyone knows that ducklings can swim and turkeys cannot," she said. "If that gray chick can't swim, then he must be a turkey."

Plip, plip, plip, plip, plip, plip went the six downy ducklings into the river. *Plop* went the gray chick. The ducklings paddled off and the gray chick followed, swimming even more gracefully than the rest.

"Goodness me!" said the mother duck again. "He must be one of us after all." But the six downy ducklings did not agree.

"You don't look like a duckling," one quacked at him.

"You're gray and ugly," quacked another. A third duckling nipped him on the neck.

"Leave him alone," said the mother duck. "It isn't his fault he looks the way he does." But the mother duck was the only one who showed any kindness to the gray chick.

In the barnyard, the other birds pulled his feathers and pecked at him every chance they got.

"You certainly don't look like your brothers and sisters," honked the goose.

"They are such beautiful ducklings," crowed the rooster. "And you are so ugly."

"Ugly duckling! Ugly duckling!" cried the other animals. From that moment on, the large gray chick was known as the Ugly Duckling. Although he tried to make the best of it, their unkind words filled his heart with sadness.

Finally one day, when he had been teased more cruelly than usual, the Ugly Duckling ran away and hid in a marsh. Beside the marsh was a small pond. It was a lonely place, but he found it very peaceful. "I will live here from now on," he decided. "If others come, I can hide in the bulrushes so they won't make fun of me."

As the days passed, birds and marsh creatures did come and go. From his hiding place in the bulrushes, the Ugly Duckling listened to them chattering happily amongst themselves. He longed to join in, but he was afraid they would mock and tease him. When the other creatures weren't around, the Ugly Duckling floated about the pond all by himself. He was so lonely that he often talked to his reflection in the water. "If only I had a friend," he sighed. "Then I would be happy, too."

One day a pair of wild ducks flew down and landed beside him. "What kind of creature are you?" asked the drake.

"I am a duckling," answered the Ugly Duckling. The drake looked surprised. "But you are so ugly!" gasped his mate.

As the Ugly Duckling hung his head in shame, the drake said, "We'll soon be heading south, where it is sunny and warm all winter. Perhaps you'd like to come with us."

"But you must promise not to marry into the family," said his mate. She shuddered at the thought of one of her pretty ducklings marrying this ugly creature.

"Thank you, but I'll stay right here," said the Ugly Duckling, for he knew that they didn't really want him.

Soon autumn came, crisp and cold. The trees along the river turned orange and red. One morning the Ugly Duckling was awakened by a strange cry. He looked up and saw a flock of snow-white birds flying overhead. The Ugly Duckling had never seen anything so magnificent. "How I wish I could fly with them," he said. "But they would never want the likes of me." Yet from that day on, the Ugly Duckling often dreamed of flying with the beautiful white birds.

Winter set in and now the land lay deep in snow. As the weather turned bitterly cold, a narrow strip of ice began to form along the edge of the pond. Slowly the ice spread until, one day, there was only a small patch of open water left. The Ugly Duckling was afraid that soon he would have nowhere left to swim, so he paddled round and round in circles to keep the ice away. By nightfall, he was too tired to climb out of the pond and take shelter in the bulrushes. In the morning, the Ugly Duckling woke to find himself frozen into the ice.

A short time later, a farmer happened to drive by on his sleigh. When he saw the poor bird, he broke the ice and took the shivering creature home to his family.

The minute the children saw the Ugly Duckling, they ran at him, shouting and laughing. They only wanted to play, but the Ugly Duckling thought they meant to hurt him. Terrified, he spread his wings and flapped about, knocking over the water bucket, breaking the milk pitcher and frightening the baby. The family chased the Ugly Duckling and shooed him right out of the house.

"Good riddance, you ugly creature!" they shouted, slamming the door behind him.

Once again the Ugly Duckling returned to the lonely pond. Somehow he managed to survive the rest of the long cold winter.

Finally spring came, and the sun began to warm the earth. As it shone down on the Ugly Duckling, he stretched toward it. A soft breeze ruffled his feathers. In pure delight, he began to fan his wings. Suddenly, wonder of wonders, he was flying! He soared through the sky, above the pond, over the farm and far, far beyond.

As the Ugly Duckling flew over a large lake, he heard a familiar cry. Looking down, he saw a flock of snow-white birds gliding across the water, their graceful necks arched. They were the same birds he had seen flying overhead in the autumn. A group of children playing by the water's edge pointed at the birds. "Look at the swans!" they shouted to one another. "Aren't they beautiful?"

"So the magnificent white birds are swans!" thought the Ugly Duckling. He flew toward them. "I don't care if they tease me or even peck me to death," he said to himself. "I want to be with them, if only for a few moments."

As he landed nearby, the swans turned to look at the newcomer. The Ugly Duckling bent his head and closed his eyes. But the blows and cruel words he expected didn't come. "Welcome, brother," said one of the swans. The others swam around the Ugly Duckling, stroking him with their bills.

"Look, a new swan!" shouted the youngest child. "And he is the most beautiful of all!"

The Ugly Duckling opened his eyes. He stared at his reflection in the water. Looking back at him was a snow-white bird, with a long graceful neck and wings that curved like giant fans.

"Could that be me?" he cried in disbelief.

Indeed it was, for during the winter the Ugly Duckling had grown into a beautiful swan. And now he had friends who welcomed him as one of their own. "I will never be lonely again," he said joyfully.

When he was a scraggly gray chick, the Ugly Duckling never dared to dream that he would become such a magnificent bird. Yet to this very day it is true that an ugly duckling can grow up to be the loveliest bird of all.

Chicken Little

One day Chicken Little was resting under a shady oak tree. Suddenly — *smack* — an acorn fell and landed on her head. "The sky is falling down!" cried Chicken Little. "What a terrible thing! I must go at once and tell the king."

So away she ran, under the fence and up the road, until she met Cocky-Locky.

"Where are you going?" asked Cocky-Locky.

"I have a terrible thing to tell the king," said Chicken Little. "The sky is falling down!"

"How do you know that?" asked Cocky-Locky.

"A piece of it fell and hit me smack on my feathery head," said Chicken Little.

"I'll come with you," said Cocky-Locky. So off ran Chicken Little and Cocky-Locky to tell the king the terrible thing — that the sky was falling down.

Away they went, over the hill and past the pond, until they met Ducky-Lucky. "Where are you rushing off to?" asked Ducky-Lucky.

"We have a terrible thing to tell the king," said Cocky-Locky. "The sky is falling down!"

"What makes you think so?" asked Ducky-Lucky.

"A piece of it fell and hit me smack on my feathery head," said Chicken Little.

"I'll come with you," said Ducky-Lucky. So off ran Chicken Little, Cocky-Locky and Ducky-Lucky to tell the king the terrible thing — that the sky was falling down.

Away they went, across the bridge and into the town, until they met Goosey-Loosey. "Where are you going in such a hurry?" asked Goosey-Loosey.

"We have a terrible thing to tell the king," said Ducky-Lucky. "The sky is falling down!"

"How do you know?" asked Goosey-Loosey.

"A piece of it fell and hit me smack on my feathery head," said Chicken Little.

"I'll come with you," said Goosey-Loosey. So off ran Chicken Little, Cocky-Locky, Ducky-Lucky and Goosey-Loosey to tell the king the terrible thing — that the sky was falling down.

Away they went, down the lane and through the park, until they met Turkey-Lurkey. "Where is everyone going?" asked Turkey-Lurkey.

"We have a terrible thing to tell the king," said Goosey-Loosey. "The sky is falling down!"

"Are you sure?" asked Turkey-Lurkey.

"A piece of it fell and hit me smack on my feathery head," said Chicken Little.

"I'll come with you," said Turkey-Lurkey. So off ran Chicken Little, Cocky-Locky, Ducky-Lucky, Goosey-Loosey and Turkey-Lurkey to tell the king the terrible thing — that the sky was falling down.

Away they went, out the gate and into the woods, until they met Foxy-Loxy. "Where are you all going?" asked Foxy-Loxy.

"We have a terrible thing to tell the king," said Turkey-Lurkey. "The sky is falling down!"

"Is it really?" asked Foxy-Loxy with a sly smile. "But this isn't the way to the king's palace. Come with me. I'll take you there myself."

"How kind of you," said Chicken Little, Cocky-Locky, Ducky-Lucky, Goosey-Loosey and Turkey-Lurkey. They all followed Foxy-Loxy to tell the king the terrible thing — that the sky was falling down.

Away they went, a long, long way, until they came to a deep dark tunnel. "This is a shortcut to the king's palace," said Foxy-Loxy. But the tunnel wasn't a shortcut to the king's palace at all. It was a shortcut to Foxy-Loxy's den.

When they reached the den, Turkey-Lurkey stepped inside. It was very dark. Suddenly, *snap!* went Foxy-Loxy's jaws. That was the end of Turkey-Lurkey.

Goosey-Loosey stepped in after him. *Snap!* went Foxy-Loxy's jaws. That was the end of Goosey-Loosey.

Ducky-Lucky stepped right in behind her. *Snap!* went Foxy-Loxy's jaws. That was the end of Ducky-Lucky.

Then Cocky-Locky stepped inside. Foxy-Loxy opened his jaws. Just as he was about to snap them shut, Cocky-Locky saw two rows of sharp shiny teeth. "Chicken Little, run for your life!" shouted Cocky-Locky.

Chicken Little turned and ran home as fast as her legs could carry her. From that day to this, Chicken Little has never had a thing to tell the king—not a single thing at all!